Mattoo, Let's Play!

For Clemente, Ruby, Mattoo and all animal friends everywhere.

Kids Can Press acknowledges the financial support of the Government of Ontario, through the Ontario Media Development Corporation's Ontario Book Initiative; the Ontario Arts Council; the Canada Council for the Arts; and the Government of Canada, through the BPIDP, for our publishing activity.

Published in Canada by
Kids Can Press Ltd.
29 Birch Avenue
Toronto, ON M4V 1E2

Published in the U.S. by
Kids Can Press Ltd.
2250 Military Road
Tonawanda, NY 14150

www.kidscanpress.com

Kids Can Press is a Corus™ Entertainment company

The artwork in this book was rendered in acrylic ink and collage.
The text is set in Grumble from Blue Vinyl Fonts.

Edited by Debbie Rogosin and Yvette Ghione
Designed by Karen Powers
Printed and bound in China

This book is smyth sewn casebound.

CM 10 0 9 8 7 6 5 4 3 2 1

LIBRARY AND ARCHIVES CANADA CATALOGUING IN PUBLICATION

Luxbacher, Irene, 1970-
    Mattoo, let's play! / written and illustrated by Irene Luxbacher.

ISBN 978-1-55453-424-1 (bound)

I. Title.

PS8623.U94M37 2010   jC813'.6   C2009-903801-3

Mattoo, Let's Play!

Written and illustrated by
IRENE LUXBACHER

Kids Can Press

My **Mattoo** is a shy cat.
He never wants to play.

I don't know why. I'm a very **friendly** person.

Want to share my balloon?

BOING! BOING!

BOING!

Ta-da!

Mattoo doesn't know
what he's missing!

I try to include Mattoo in my favorite
games, like **Space Flight** to **Pluto.**

C'mon, Mattoo.
Let's chase the dog star!

MEOW?

Darn. We didn't even get to taste the Milky Way.

Here you go, Mattoo. Bon appétit!

I even prepare **lunch** for Mattoo: a chocolate sundae and triple-decker jelly sandwiches — my speciality!

RESERVED

Mattoo   Ruby

GASP!

But Mattoo doesn't like my cooking.

I don't think Mattoo will **ever** play with me.

My friend **Clemente** is always happy to play.
So one day, after a flight on our jet-propelled
scooters, Clemente and I land deep in the jungle.
"Let's go on **safari!**" I say.

While Clemente builds a camp,
I make my **loudest** wild elephant call ever!

TOOOOT!

We **wait**, and **watch**,
and whisper.

I think I see
something.

Me, too!

Just when we think we've seen
every amazing animal, we notice
something strange moving
toward us.

It's the **fiercest**, most wild, most wonderful
creature of all — the **mysterious** spotted
king of the **jungle!**

Be carefull

Cool!

To show that we're friendly, we carefully give the wild beast some tuna snacks and gently pat its fuzzy mane.

Prrrrrrrrrrrrrrrr

It isn't long before
the rare jungle cat
is as playful as
a **kitten**.

My Mattoo is a ~~shy~~ playful cat.
We sure know how to have a good time!

Prrrrrrrr